To Kimberly

Enjoy!

Emily's Secret

Ruth McKeague

Ruth McKeague

Illustrated by Shelley Durling

Essence
PUBLISHING

Belleville, Ontario, Canada

Acknowledgements & Dedication

I would like to thank the following people for the valuable help they have offered in order to make this book a reality:

Paul McKeague, my brother, for his thorough editing work;

David Spence, of the Wild Bird Care Centre of Nepean, Ontario, for sharing his expertise on Canada geese;

Pastor Stephen Elliott, of Kanata Wesleyan Church, for the initiatives he took leading to the publication of *Emily's Secret*;

Bonnie Shea, of the Kanata Wesleyan Church, for her advice and coaching in the preparation of the Bible study for *Emily's Secret*;

David Gardner, my husband, for the support and direction he gave to help me see the dream of this book come true.

This book is dedicated, with motherly love, to
Rachael Gardner

Printed in Canada
by

Essence
PUBLISHING

Emily's Secret

"We are at Black Lake at last," wrote Emily in her diary as soon as the tent trailer was set up. *"Mom would **kill** me if she knew I ate the chocolate bars in the car...."*

"Emily?" It was Mom.

"Yes?"

Quickly, Emily shut her diary and stuffed it back into her bag of clothes. Mom's head popped through the trailer door.

"I'm so tired," groaned Emily.

"Dad and I need your help, Em. We're going to put up the kitchen tent and somebody has to look after Davey."

Emily rolled her eyes back. "I said I was tired, Mom."

"I know, Emily, and we're *all* tired – believe me. But there's work to be done, so let's do it. Come on now, be a big girl."

"Be a big girl, be a big girl," thought Emily to herself as she got up.

Outside, Mom and Dad were staring at the poles for the new kitchen tent. They seemed confused. Emily took her little brother by the hand and went to the rock that was on their camp site. From there, they could see all of Black Lake.

"See Davey? There's the beach. You played on it last year – but you can't remember because you were only one. It's all made out of sand," she explained.

"Shaaand," Davey said very seriously.

"And there's the water. See the people swimming?"

"Sim sim!"

"And there's the raft where I always dive. You're too little for that. And there's the marsh with the cattails, right at the side of the beach, and..." Emily stopped for a moment.

In the marsh, two geese were paddling around, hidden from the view of the swimmers on the beach.

"Mom and Dad, look at the geese!" shouted Emily, "Remember my project on the Canada goose in Mrs. Henderson's class? I got the highest mark in...."

"*Emily*, we're setting up the kitchen tent." Mom sounded so annoyed. "We'll look around when we have time."

Emily bit her bottom lip. *"Mrs. Henderson gave me an A+ on that project,"* she thought to herself.

"What was it you saw when you were on the rock, Em?" asked Mom as the family ate a quick dinner of hot dogs at the picnic table.

"Geese."

"Oh yes," said Dad, "I've seen lots of geese on these lakes. But *I* always liked the loons. Can you pass the mustard, Em? No, no, Davey! Don't *do* that with your food!"

Emily passed the mustard. *"I hope we'll go to the beach after supper so that I can see them,"* she thought.

After supper, Emily's family did go down to the beach.

"I'll have you a race into the water, Mom and Dad."

Mom lay down on her towel. "You go on ahead, Em. I'm wiped out."

"Yes, go on ahead," said Dad. He was helping Davey fill up his pail with sand.

Emily went into the water alone. She closed her eyes, took a deep breath, dove right under, and glided as far as she could. When she came up again, she stretched her arms straight up into the air. How good it was to be here!

Emily remembered the geese. She wandered over to the marsh, and as she came closer, she stepped more gently. They were still there!

"Canada geese!" she thought. She recognized them right away. *"The one with the tall straight neck is the male – the gander."* Emily thought of Mrs. Henderson. She couldn't wait to tell her about this! *"That one is female – the goose. She's got a curved neck and...."*

Then she saw it. The geese had a nest! It was at the bottom of the dry old tree standing at the edge of the marsh. Emily's mouth and eyes grew wide. Yes, the mother goose was sitting on a nest! She looked like a queen on her throne. Emily stepped closer. The gander's head started to bob up and down, and he wove nervously among the cattails. Then, both he and the goose lowered their heads to the water. Emily stepped back a bit to calm them, and just looked on very quietly.

"You're protecting your wife and your babies, aren't you?" she thought as she smiled at the male. *"You're a good daddy."*

The mother goose raised her head and stood up for a moment to turn around. As she did, Emily saw four eggs. *"Wow!"*

Emily tiptoed back a bit, and then turned to look at her own family. Mom was helping Dad and Davey build a sandcastle.

*"She's not too wiped out to play with **him**,"* Emily noticed.

She turned back again to face the water. Nobody else knew. She was the only one.

Later that evening, as Davey slept beside her in the tent trailer, Emily pulled out her diary and her flashlight.

"I wonder when they'll hatch..." she wrote.

Very early the next morning, when no one else was awake, Emily slipped outside. How were the geese? How were those eggs doing? She *had* to find out! Without making a sound, she put on her running shoes and crept off the campsite. First stop was the outhouse. Then, the beach!

The mother goose was standing in her nest, running her beak up long blades of grass and eating their seeds at the top. Emily looked at the eggs and gasped. There were little cracks appearing around each one! *"They **are** going to hatch soon!"*

The mother goose sat down again. Emily just stood still. Soon, she heard murmuring sounds. She knew what they were! Those sounds from the mother could be heard by the goslings, still in their shells. Emily kept listening. Sure enough, she heard the high-pitched murmuring of the goslings. *"Awesome!"* They were murmuring to each other, getting ready to break out of their shells – all at the same time.

Emily's face was bright. *She* knew what was happening in that nest! A whole new family was coming to life! It was like watching a miracle.

Emily stepped a little closer. Then, she noticed that something was different. The goose was all by herself. When she saw Emily, she squawked and laid her head low upon the water's surface, unprotected and alone. Emily wondered where the gander could be. Maybe out getting some food?

"He'll be back soon," she whispered to the mother goose.

From across the lake came the voices of campers waking up. It was time to go back.

Mom had come out of the trailer. She was stretching when Emily arrived back at the campsite. "Good morning, Emily," she said, "Were you at the outhouse?"

Emily nodded.

"Please don't go out alone, Em. Just wake me up when you have to go, OK?" Mom had a slow, tired smile that made Emily feel good. "I was having such a delicious sleep that I didn't even hear you get out of the trailer," she yawned, "What we *all* heard was the kitchen tent collapsing."

"Oh no," groaned Emily. The kitchen tent was swaying, with Dad holding it up from the inside.

"Cheryl," came his frustrated voice, "do you know where that instruction sheet is?"

By the time Dad sat down at the picnic table, Mom, Emily and Davey had almost finished breakfast.

"That should do it," he mumbled. His eyebrows were tight.

Mom passed him his favourite cereal. "I'm sure there's someone around who could give us a hand if we need help," she said.

"It's fine," Dad grunted.

Emily patiently collected rocks with Davey while her parents cleaned the breakfast dishes.

"*Big* rock," said Davey very wisely as he picked up a large grey stone.

"Yes," Emily said, "that's a *very* big rock. Can you find me a little rock?"

Davey put his finger in his mouth and studied the ground. All at once, his finger flew up in the air, sloppy and wet.

"Little rock! Teeny, weeny rock! See, Emwee?"

Emily took the small white stone from his hands. "Good for you, Davey."

"I hope," she thought, *"that the gander is back."*

Mom and Dad had finished the dishes.

"Can we go to the beach now?" Emily asked them.

"This morning, we're going for a hike, Em," said Dad. He kept turning his head to check the kitchen tent.

"Can I go down to the beach and just wait for you there before we go?"

"I don't see why not..." started Dad. "Emily, your shoes are wet. How did they get wet? You *can't* hike in those."

Emily tensed up. "Oh, I... I...."

"Relax, Doug – she's a child," said Mom, "Your other shoes are in the trailer, Em. Get them on and leave those wet ones in the sun to dry, OK? You'll get sores on your feet if you hike in wet shoes."

Emily felt relieved. "OK," she said.

A few morning swimmers were on the beach now. Emily took off her shoes and waded in among the cattails. What she saw in the nest made her heart pound. The goslings were out of their shells! What a colour they were! Yellow-green... like the grass in the backyard when Dad lifted up the sand box. The down on their tiny bodies looked like gelled hair that puffed out as it dried. They huddled closely around the mother goose. *"They look so cozy,"* thought Emily. She just wanted to hug....

"Emily, get your shoes on." It was Dad. He was coming down the path with Mom and Davey.

Emily noticed that the gander was still missing.

*"Where **is** he? Why is he taking so long?"*

The mother goose bobbed her head nervously before she laid it low to the water.

"Come on, Em!" Dad sounded impatient.

Emily walked quietly along beside her father on the hiking trail. Mom was up ahead with Davey on her shoulders. Emily could hear her talking to Davey. They stopped when they reached the look-out.

"It says here that this is the best view around," said Dad, looking at a booklet. "I guess we should have our snack here."

"Wow!" whispered Mom. The lake, the beach, another lake, little islands, trees – you could see everything from the look-out. "Whoever made all this sure did a good job. Don't you think so, Em?"

Emily looked at the beach. It seemed so small from the look-out. The marsh looked like a patch of grass. She wondered if the goslings were alright. How she longed to be with them!

As they finished their snack, the wind started to blow and clouds moved to cover the sun. Mom and Dad said it was time to go back.

Emily's step quickened as her family neared the end of the hike. Soon, they'd be crossing the beach again.

"Can I run up ahead?" she asked Dad.

"Sure," he said.

Emily raced forward. There were no swimmers left on the beach. The wind was blowing hard now, and it looked like it would rain soon.

All of a sudden, Emily heard a startled cry from the marsh. She looked up. What was that scruffy-looking creature? A fox? It stopped and stared at her before scampering away with something big in its mouth. What was going on? Emily gasped for breath. Something was terribly wrong.

She stopped at the water's edge by the marsh. It was hard to see, but she peered right through the cattails to the spot where the nest was. The goslings were all alone! *"The fox took the mother away!"* Emily realized in despair. The four baby birds looked so helpless. Their heads were up as they peeped for their mother. Emily grabbed her hair. *"Now they have **nobody** to look after them."* She wanted to scream.

"Emily!" Dad sounded so irritated. "Did you step in the water with *those* shoes too?"

"No!" yelled Emily angrily. A drop of rain fell on her as she started to run.

"Doug, you've *got* to loosen up! We're on vacation. Don't *ruin* it for everyone!"

Emily ran ahead of her family back to the campsite. Would the goslings get cold in the wind? Would they get sick in the rain? Would they get hungry all alone?

The kitchen tent had collapsed again.

"Oh, no!" groaned Dad.

Mom put her arm around Dad's shoulder. Emily took Davey into the trailer and lay down beside him as he napped. The rain fell loudly on the roof above her. Mom was talking outside.

"Doug, I'm feeling so badly for Emily. You've been hard on her. I'm sorry for snapping at you down at the beach though – that was wrong of me...."

"You've got nothing to apologize for, Cheryl," said Dad. "I've been all stressed out, and I know I've been too hard on Emily...."

"Geese have feathers that protect them from the rain and water," thought Emily, staring at the ceiling of the trailer. *"But I don't know if goslings do. I don't* **know***!"* When she closed her eyes, a tear rolled out.

Mom was giggling.

"And if it ever dries up," Dad was shouting, "We are going to *burn* this tent and roast marshmallows over it!"

"This rain is hurting them." Emily tossed and turned. *"It's coming down too hard – it might kill them."*

Dad was singing. "Rain drops keep falling on my head..."

"Please God," Emily prayed as the tears streamed down her face, *"let them live."*

Mom was howling with laughter.

"I love you, Cheryl."

She held the umbrella and stood on the sand. She stepped as close as she could to the water's edge without getting her shoes wet. She stretched her arm out, trying to protect the goslings from the rain with her umbrella. But she couldn't do it! Her arms were too short! The rain was hitting the goslings sharply. They cried out. Emily panicked. "I want to help you," she screamed. "HELP...!"

"Emily!" Dad was dripping wet, "It's a dream, Honey. It's OK, you're alright."

Emily was trembling and pale.

"What was it, Sweetheart?" Mom looked alarmed.

"There were goslings born in the marsh this morning and they're all alone. Their dad is gone and their mom got taken away by a fox," she sobbed. "They might die in this rain. They need help."

Davey rolled over and sat up with a cranky whine.

"What can we do?" Mom asked Dad.

"I could go ask the people at the park office. They might know."

Emily's eyes were big and sad. "Maybe we could put the umbrella over them."

"What a great idea," said Dad gently.

Mom grabbed their big black umbrella. "Let's go now, Em."

It was like she was flying. The rain just soaked her as she ran to the beach. Emily felt a pounding joy! Mom was just up ahead with the umbrella. Emily ran faster.

They walked right into the water without taking their shoes off. Splish, splash, splosh. Right up to their knees.

"Oh, Emily!" Mom was seeing the goslings for the first time. They were all fine, protected by the cattails. Rain water dripped on their downy feathers gently as it rolled off the flat leaves of the marsh. The goslings were stumbling about in their nest, going in all directions. They looked like confused shoppers in a crowded mall.

Emily looked up at her mom and put her arms around her waist. It rained, and rained, and rained.

"Mom?" said Emily.

"Yes, Em?"

"I ate the chocolate bars in the car."

Mom had to think for a moment. "Oh, *Emily!*" she scolded. "Your allowance buys the replacements, young lady."

Emily hugged her mom tighter.

A big red umbrella was wobbling down the path that led to the beach. Dad, Davey and a man from the park office were underneath it. Mom waved to them and signalled that the goslings were OK.

"See, Davey," whispered Dad when they had stepped into the water, "those are goslings. They're baby geese."

Davey put his finger in his mouth and just stared.

The man from the park office had a metal name tag pinned to his shirt that said 'John Dubois: Park Warden.'

"It would be better to protect the goslings in some other way," he said as he pulled a big piece of loose bark away from the old elm tree by the nest. "If the parents do come back, they won't recognize the nest if it's got an umbrella over it." John Dubois set the bark up beside the nest, and let it lean against the tree. "They won't like seeing *us* here either," he explained as he led the way back to the beach.

"What about food?" asked Mom. "The goslings must be hungry."

"Goslings don't need to eat anything for the first twenty-four hours," John explained. "If the parents haven't returned by the morning, we'll make sure they're fed."

"I hate to leave them alone until the morning," Mom said. "Isn't there anything we can do?"

"You've already done all that can be done for now. They needed protection from the rain, and thanks to you, they have it."

All of a sudden, Dad gasped. In amazement, he pointed at something – something waddling close to the water's edge.

"The mother goose!" whispered Emily, clutching her father's hand.

Everyone stood very still. The goose limped awkwardly across the sand with a heavy tiredness.

"Her wing looks hurt," said Dad.

The goose got to the water and paddled right up to the nest. Her goslings burrowed down underneath her. She nestled in peacefully, and tended to her injured wing. Whatever she had gone through, she was home – she had made it. Emily felt so happy.

"The fox gave her a good fight," said John, "but she gave the fox an even better fight."

Everyone looked hopefully across the beach and the lake, waiting for the gander to return too, but he didn't.

"I wonder if a fox..." thought Emily sadly as she looked for him. But she didn't want to think about it.

"Goosees!" yelled Davey.

"That's right," said Mom, "but we can't go see them now, Davey. Their mommy is back! Isn't that great?"

"Goosees! Go see gooseeeees!" he shouted.

"We'd better go," said Mom.

The warden nodded his head and waved good-bye. Mom stretched out her arms for Davey, and Dad took the black umbrella. He put his arm around Emily, and all in a huddle, the family walked back up to their campsite.

Dad grinned at Mom. "John fixed the kitchen tent while we were up there," he said. "He made it look so easy."

Mom made a funny face, pretending to look surprised. "Isn't it *amazing* what can happen when we ask for help?" she said, nudging Dad's shoulder.

Dad nudged back and just kept grinning.

"Gooseeeeeeeees!" wailed Davey all the way.

Emily and her parents stayed up by the fire long after supper; long after Davey had gone to bed.

"You mean you actually *heard* the goslings in their shells?" asked Dad.

Emily was eager for Dad's questions. "It was easier to hear them than the goose even," she said with wide eyes staring right at him.

"But how do you know they were talking about breaking out of their shells?"

"Because that's what geese do! I even saw the cracks in the eggs – they were getting ready to break out alright. And goslings all come out of their shells at the same time."

"They can swim almost right away," said Mom, "can't they, Em?"

"Yep."

"Tell Dad why they lay their heads flat on the water."

"Geese have a white patch under their heads," she said excitedly, "and when they don't want to be seen, they hide it in the water. Do you know what I mean? When the white patch is hidden, they're harder to see."

"I know what you mean," smiled Dad. "Honey, did you ever tell me about this project you did?"

"I don't know..." shrugged Emily.

"I'm sure we told you about it," said Mom. "Remember when I drove Emily to the library that time?"

Dad nodded his head silently. His face had a sad, far away look.

After a while, the fire in the fireplace went out. Emily became so tired, she could hardly hold up her head.

"I'm going to bed now," she mumbled. "Good night, Mom and Dad."

"Good night, Emily," said Mom, giving her a kiss.

Dad put his arms around Emily and gave her a big hug. "You're a smart girl, Emily," he said in a quiet voice. "I'll want to hear about all your projects from now on, OK?"

Emily nodded her head against her father's shoulder, and fell asleep.

Early the next morning, Emily woke up in the tent trailer. She peeked outside and was surprised to see Dad walking towards the campsite from the beach. He had a feather in his hand. Emily stepped outside to see him.

"Come over here, Em!" he said as he hurried over to the rock, "I went down to check on the geese, but they were all swimming away. Look who's back."

He was pointing to a line of birds paddling across the lake. Emily counted them: four small ones, and *two* big ones.

"The father – the gander!" Emily exclaimed, "He came back!"

"He sure did."

"Did he seem OK? Do you think he got hurt by a fox?"

"I couldn't tell," said Dad with a shrug, "but he seemed pretty glad to be back with his family." Dad nodded his head, "I bet they're looking for a new home now. They've had bad luck in that marsh."

"Aw," sighed Emily. She wished they would stay.

"The timing was right, Emily. They were on the beach when they needed our help, and now, it's best for them to move on – to get away from it all and have a fresh start."

"I'll miss them," said Emily.

"Me too," said Dad. He held up the feather. "When I was down there, I found this on the beach. Don't you think we should keep it, Em... so that we can remember them?"

Emily took the feather and thought, *"A book mark for my diary...."*

"I was thinking," continued Dad, "that it would be nice to put it in our photo album – right in with the pictures from this camping trip."

Emily's smile shone as she looked up at her Dad. "OK," she said. "Can I show Mom?"

"Sure," he said. "It's time those sleepyheads got up out of bed."

Emily ran to the trailer with her father close behind. And the line of birds paddling across the lake became thinner and thinner, as the Canada geese went in search of a new home.